# Race Car is Roaring

Mandy Archer

Illustrated by Martha Lightfoot

NEW
BURLINGTON
BOOKS

Rabbit opens the **workshop** doors.

Race Car **shines brightly** in the morning sunshine.

A **mechanic** tops up Race Car's **oil**.
Another checks its **engine** on
a special **computer**.

There are just a **few hours** to go
until the **big race!**

Rabbit **zips** up his **coveralls.**

He climbs into the **cockpit.**

Rabbit **gently steers**
Race Car onto the track.

VVRROOOMMM

VVRROOOMMM

The **team** take its places
on the **starting grid**.

The mechanics make their
**last-minute** checks.

Rabbit gives the **thumbs-up**.
Race Car is **ready!**

The Marshall clears the track.
The start lights glow red one by one.

Rabbit shifts gears and pushes pedals.

WHOOSH!

Race Car screeches around the first bend. The crowd cheers.

Rabbit takes a **tricky turn**
at **top speed.**

A yellow car suddenly appears
in Race Car's **mirror.**
It's trying to **overtake!**

**SCREECH!**

The yellow car goes too fast and **skids** onto the **gravel** at the side of the track.

No one can **catch** Rabbit and Race Car now!

Race Car **completes** another lap and then another.

The Team Manager uses the radio system to call Rabbit in for a **pit stop**.

New **tires** are quickly **fitted** to Race Car.

Car after car streaks past.
Rabbit watches them go.

The cars **tear down** the home **stretch**.
Race Car is in **first** place!

But suddenly Rabbit
leans forward.

What's that
up ahead?

The crowd gasps. There's an **oil spill** on the track!

Race Car is **zooming** closer and closer.

Rabbit **grips** the **steering wheel**.

Rabbit swerves around the slippery oil.

SCREECH!

Race Car is safe!
The Marshall waves a flag to warn the other drivers.

The race is still on, but there can only be one **winner**.

Race Car **ZOOMS** past the **checkered flag**, in first place.

HOORAY! HOORAY! HOORAY! HOORAY!

Rabbit climbs onto the winner's podium.
He lifts the trophy and smiles.

Well done, Race Car. You're a champion!

# Let's look at
# Race Car

Engine

Rear
wing

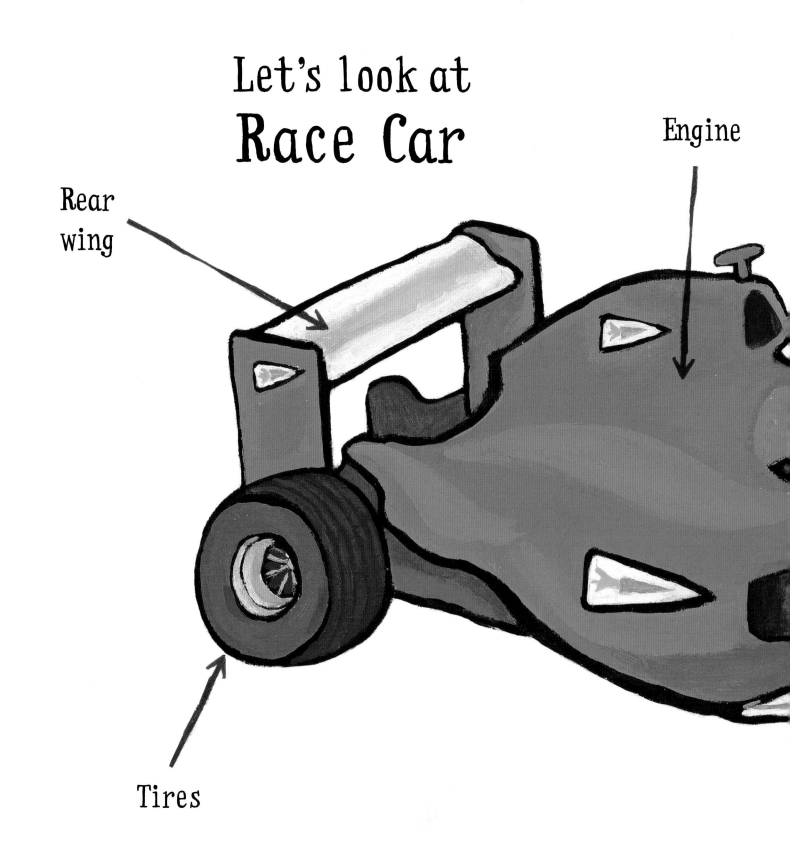

Tires

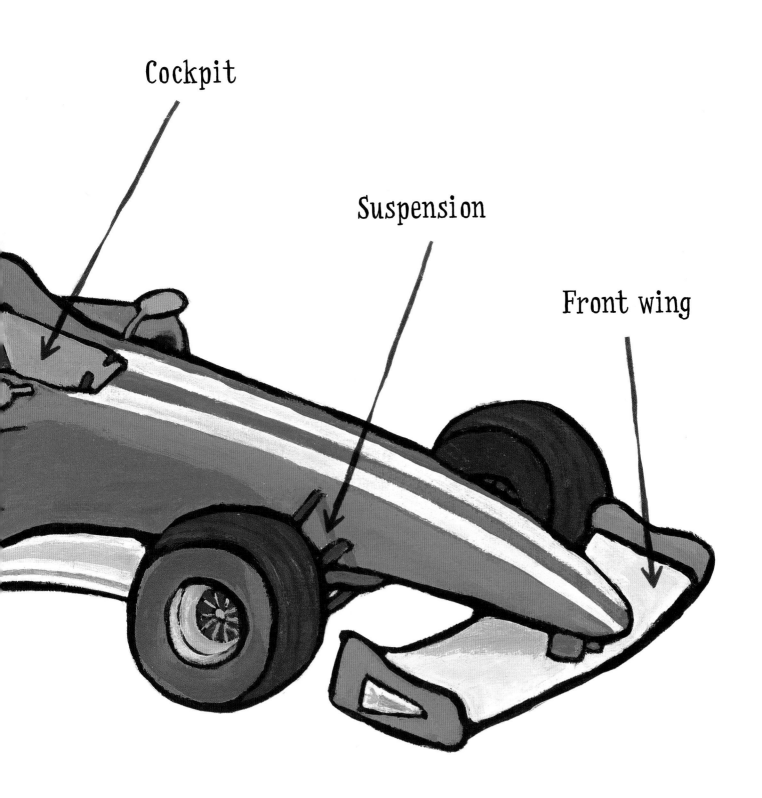

Cockpit

Suspension

Front wing

# Racing Machines

## Motorcycle

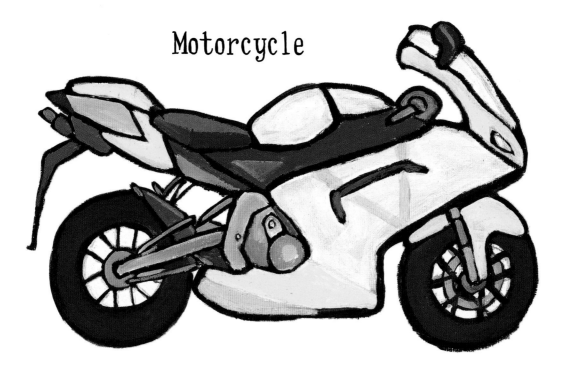

## NASCAR race car

Formula One car

Rally car

For Pete M.L.

A NEW BURLINGTON BOOK
The Old Brewery
6 Blundell Street
London N7 9BH

Designer: Plum Pudding Design

Copyright © QEB Publishing 2012

First published in the United States in 2012 by
QEB Publishing, Inc.
3 Wrigley, Suite A
Irvine, CA 92618

www.qed-publishing.co.uk

A CIP record for this book is available from the Library of Congress.

ISBN: 978 1 78171 391 4

Printed in China